THE BLANK BOOK

✳ **A Series of Unfortunate Events** ✳

THE BLANK BOOK

Illustrations by **Brett Helquist**

■ *HARPERCOLLINSPublishers*

✳

❖

THE BLANK BOOK

The sad truth is that the truth is sad.
—THE CARNIVOROUS CARNIVAL

A new experience can be extremely pleasurable, or
extremely irritating, or somewhere in between, and you
never know until you try it out.
—THE MISERABLE MILL

"People don't always get what they deserve in this world."
—Esmé Squalor, THE CARNIVOROUS CARNIVAL

It is always cruel to laugh at people, of course,
although sometimes if they are wearing an ugly hat
it is hard to control yourself.
—THE AUSTERE ACADEMY

The key to good eavesdropping is not getting caught.
—THE REPTILE ROOM

It is terribly rude to tell people
that their troubles are boring.
—THE ERSATZ ELEVATOR

Whenever you are examining someone else's belongings,
you are bound to learn many interesting things about the
person of which you were not previously aware.
—THE CARNIVOROUS CARNIVAL

To hear the phrase "our only hope" always makes one
anxious, because it means that if the only hope doesn't
work, there is nothing left. —THE ERSATZ ELEVATOR

Just because you don't understand
it doesn't mean it isn't so.
—THE BAD BEGINNING

Like a church bell, a coffin, and a vat of melted chocolate, a supply closet is rarely a comfortable place to hide.
—THE HOSTILE HOSPITAL

Oftentimes, when people are miserable, they will want to
make other people miserable, too. But it never helps.
—THE WIDE WINDOW

Even though there is no way of knowing for sure,
there are often ways to know for pretty sure.
—THE VILE VILLAGE

You would run much slower if you were
dragging something behind you,
like a knapsack or a sheriff.
—THE SLIPPERY SLOPE

Morning is an important time of day, because how you spend your morning can often tell you what kind of day you are going to have. —THE MISERABLE MILL

"Criminals should be punished, not fed pastries."
—Lou, THE HOSTILE HOSPITAL

If you are trying to fool a farsighted or dimwitted person,
a veiled facial disguise might be enough.
—*V.F.D. Disguise Training manual,*
LEMONY SNICKET: THE UNAUTHORIZED AUTOBIOGRAPHY

Just because something is traditional is no reason to do it,
of course. —THE AUSTERE ACADEMY

It is very unnerving to be proven wrong,
particularly when you are really right and the person
who is really wrong is the one who is proving you wrong
and proving himself, wrongly, right. —THE REPTILE ROOM

Certain words make you think of certain things, even if you
don't want to. —THE HOSTILE HOSPITAL

Unless you have been very, very lucky, you know that a
good, long session of weeping can often make you feel
better, even if your circumstances have not changed one bit.
—THE BAD BEGINNING

When one's stomach is as fluttery as all that,
it is nice to take a short break to lie down
and perhaps sip a fizzy beverage.
—THE VILE VILLAGE

Unlike babies, citizens, and moths, leeches are quite
unpleasant to begin with. —THE WIDE WINDOW

"It's a little confusing pretending to be
a completely different person."
—Violet Baudelaire, THE CARNIVOROUS CARNIVAL

Deciding on the right thing to do is a bit like deciding on
the right thing to wear to a party. It is easy to
decide on what is wrong to wear to a party, such as
deep-sea diving equipment or a pair of large pillows,
but deciding what is right is much trickier.
—THE SLIPPERY SLOPE

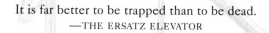

It is far better to be trapped than to be dead.
—THE ERSATZ ELEVATOR

There are two basic types of panicking: standing still and not saying a word, and leaping all over the place babbling anything that comes into your head. —THE REPTILE ROOM

"It may take a village to raise a child, but it only takes one
child to inherit a fortune."
—Detective Dupin, THE VILE VILLAGE

Besides occasionally wearing an ugly yellow coat, the worst a realtor can do is show you a house that you find ugly, and so it is completely irrational to be terrified of them.
—THE WIDE WINDOW

"In certain cases, enthusiasm can make up for a lack of brainpower." —Coach Genghis, THE AUSTERE ACADEMY

A miserable experience remains a miserable experience
even on the loveliest of mornings. —THE MISERABLE MILL

Eavesdropping is a valuable thing to do, and it is often an enjoyable thing to do, but it is not a polite thing to do, and like most impolite things, you are bound to get into trouble if you get caught doing it. —THE CARNIVOROUS CARNIVAL

First impressions are often entirely wrong.
—THE BAD BEGINNING

One of the easiest ways to avoid the attention of one's
enemies is to concoct a long, false tale about how
something was passed to you by a mysterious stranger.
—Daniel Handler, Introduction to LEMONY SNICKET:
THE UNAUTHORIZED AUTOBIOGRAPHY

"MURDERER ATTEMPTS
TO MURDER MURDERER"
—Headline from *The Daily Punctilio*,
THE HOSTILE HOSPITAL

Bad circumstances have a way of ruining things that would otherwise be pleasant. —THE REPTILE ROOM

When someone tells you to do something unusual without
an explanation, it is very difficult not to ask why.
—THE SLIPPERY SLOPE

"There is something illegal about dangling
an infant out of a tower window."
—Justice Strauss, THE BAD BEGINNING

Gluing things to a door is never
a very exciting thing to watch.
—THE ERSATZ ELEVATOR

If you are a student you should always get a good night's sleep unless you have come to the good part of your book, and then you should stay up all night and let your schoolwork fall by the wayside, a phrase which means "flunk."
—THE AUSTERE ACADEMY

The quoting of an aphorism, like the angry barking of a dog
or the smell of overcooked broccoli, rarely indicates that
something helpful is about to happen. —THE VILE VILLAGE

Taking one's chances is like taking a bath, because
sometimes you end up feeling comfortable and warm, and
sometimes there is something terrible lurking around that
you cannot see until it is too late and you can do nothing
else but scream and cling to a plastic duck.
—THE SLIPPERY SLOPE

If you are allergic to a thing, it is best not to put that thing
in your mouth, particularly if the thing is cats.
—THE WIDE WINDOW

It is hard for decent people to stay angry at someone who has burst into tears, which is why it is often a good idea to burst into tears if a decent person is yelling at you.
—THE CARNIVOROUS CARNIVAL

If you are expecting someone at a certain time and they have not shown up, it is difficult to know exactly when to give up and decide they are not coming.

—LEMONY SNICKET: THE UNAUTHORIZED AUTOBIOGRAPHY

Unfortunate things can happen to celery as easily as they can happen to children. —THE AUSTERE ACADEMY

At the moment, they knew nothing of the troubles ahead of them, only of the troubles behind them, and the troubles that had escaped out the window. —THE MISERABLE MILL

In life it is often the tiny details that end up
being the most important. —THE REPTILE ROOM

When you read as many books as Klaus Baudelaire, you are going to learn a great deal of information that might not become useful for a long time. —THE HOSTILE HOSPITAL

There is nothing particularly wrong with salmon, of course, but like caramel candy, strawberry yogurt, and liquid carpet cleaner, if you eat too much of it you are not going to enjoy your meal. —THE ERSATZ ELEVATOR

Wishing is merely a quiet way to spend one's time before
the candles are extinguished on one's birthday cake.
—THE SLIPPERY SLOPE

The worst surroundings in the world can be tolerated if the
people in them are interesting and kind.
—THE BAD BEGINNING

Shyness is a curious thing, because, like quicksand, it can strike people at any time, and also, like quicksand, it usually makes its victims look down. —THE AUSTERE ACADEMY

A good library will never be too neat, or too dusty, because somebody will always be in it, taking books off the shelves and staying up late reading them. —THE ERSATZ ELEVATOR

If you know somebody very well, like your grandmother or
your baby sister, you will know when they are real and
when they are fake. —THE REPTILE ROOM

"Slow service is one of the disadvantages of having infants for slaves."—Count Olaf, THE SLIPPERY SLOPE

No matter who you are, no matter where you live, and no matter how many people are chasing you, what you don't read is often as important as what you do read.
—THE VILE VILLAGE

On a cold day, in a drafty room, chilled cucumber soup is about as welcome as a swarm of wasps at a bat mitzvah.

—THE WIDE WINDOW

It is hard to think about mysteries and secrets first thing in the morning, particularly if someone is yelling at you.
—THE SLIPPERY SLOPE

Sometimes, when you are reading a book you are
enjoying very much, you begin thinking so hard
about the characters and the story that you might
forget all about the author, even if he is in grave danger
and would very much appreciate your help.
—LEMONY SNICKET: THE UNAUTHORIZED AUTOBIOGRAPHY

"The world is a harum-scarum place."
—Olivia, THE CARNIVOROUS CARNIVAL

Everybody will die, but very few people want to be reminded of that fact. —THE AUSTERE ACADEMY

Raisins are healthy, and they are inexpensive, and some people may even find them delicious. But they are rarely considered helpful. —THE MISERABLE MILL

Morning is one of the best times for thinking. When one has just woken up, but hasn't yet gotten out of bed, it is a perfect time to look up at the ceiling, consider one's life, and wonder what the future will hold.

—THE ERSATZ ELEVATOR

"Sometimes the information you need is not
in the most obvious place." —Hal, THE HOSTILE HOSPITAL

In this book, not only is there no happy ending,
there is no happy beginning and very few happy things
happen in the middle. —THE BAD BEGINNING

Normally it is not polite to go into somebody's room without knocking, but you can make an exception if the person is dead, or pretending to be dead. —THE WIDE WINDOW

It is better not to make too many assumptions, particularly in the morning. —THE AUSTERE ACADEMY

Sometimes even in the most unfortunate of lives there will
occur a moment or two of good fortune.
—THE REPTILE ROOM

It is never a good idea to stand around a flat and empty landscape while the police are closing in to arrest you for a crime you have not committed. —THE HOSTILE HOSPITAL

"If everyone fought fire with fire, the entire world would go up in smoke."—Violet Baudelaire, THE SLIPPERY SLOPE

Although "jumping to conclusions" is an expression, rather than an activity, it is as dangerous as jumping off a cliff, jumping in front of a moving train, and jumping for joy.
—THE VILE VILLAGE

It is much, much worse to receive bad news through the written word than by somebody simply telling you.
—THE MISERABLE MILL

"There is no worse sound in the world than someone who cannot play the violin who insists on doing so anyway."
—Violet, Klaus, and Sunny Baudelaire's father,
THE AUSTERE ACADEMY

Arguing with somebody is never pleasant, but sometimes it is useful and necessary to do so. —THE ERSATZ ELEVATOR

One of the most troublesome things in life is that what you
do or do not want has very little to do with what does or
does not happen. —THE CARNIVOROUS CARNIVAL

"It doesn't take courage to kill someone.
It takes a severe lack of moral stamina."
—Klaus Baudelaire, THE HOSTILE HOSPITAL

Unless you are a lightbulb, an electrical appliance, or a tree that is tired of standing upright, encountering a bolt from the blue is not a pleasant experience. —THE VILE VILLAGE

When you have only known someone for a few hours
it is difficult to know what they would like to hear.
—THE WIDE WINDOW

Miracles are like meatballs, because nobody can exactly agree what they are made of, where they come from, or how often they should appear. —THE CARNIVOROUS CARNIVAL

Fate is like a strange, unpopular restaurant filled with odd
waiters who bring you things you never asked for
and don't always like. —THE SLIPPERY SLOPE

Troublesome things tend to remain troublesome
no matter how many times you do them.
—THE ERSATZ ELEVATOR

"Siblings must take care of one another when they
are all alone in the world." —Sally Sebald,
LEMONY SNICKET: THE UNAUTHORIZED AUTOBIOGRAPHY

Hedge clippers and a plastic bag are not
appropriate methods of greeting someone, of course,
particularly first thing in the morning. —THE VILE VILLAGE

One of the most difficult things to think about in life is
one's regrets. —THE REPTILE ROOM

Just about everything in this world is easier said than done,
with the exception of "systematically assisting
Sisyphus's stealthy cyst-susceptible sister,"
which is easier done than said.
—THE HOSTILE HOSPITAL

From time to time, the Baudelaire children looked at one
another, but with their future such a mystery they could
think of nothing to say. —THE BAD BEGINNING

"Nothing spoils a nice car trip
like a whiny kidnapping victim."
—Count Olaf, THE SLIPPERY SLOPE

Whenever there is a mirror around, it is almost impossible
not to take a look at yourself. Even though we all know
what we look like, we all like just to look at our reflections,
if only to see how we're doing. —THE MISERABLE MILL

"Dominoes is a game. Water polo is a game.
Murder is a crime, and you will go to jail for it."
—Mr. Poe, THE REPTILE ROOM

If you've ever dressed up for Halloween
or attended a masquerade, you know that
there is a certain thrill to wearing a disguise.
—THE AUSTERE ACADEMY

I feel as if my whole life has been nothing but a dismal play, presented just for someone else's amusement, and that the playwright who invented my cruel twist of fate is somewhere far above me, laughing and laughing at his creation.

—THE HOSTILE HOSPITAL

There are few sights sadder than a ruined book.
—THE WIDE WINDOW

Sometimes, when someone tells a ridiculous lie,
it is best to ignore it entirely.
—THE REPTILE ROOM

A library is normally a very good place to work in the
afternoon, but not if its window has been smashed
and there is a hurricane approaching.
—THE WIDE WINDOW

Grinning is something you do when you are entertained in some way, such as reading a good book or watching someone you don't care for spill orange soda all over himself.
—THE VILE VILLAGE

There are many things in life that become different
if you take a long look at them.
—THE CARNIVOROUS CARNIVAL

If you refuse to entertain a baby cousin,
the baby cousin may get bored and entertain itself
by wandering off and falling down a well.
—THE VILE VILLAGE

There is usually no reason to be afraid of the dark,
but even if you are not particularly afraid of something,
you might not want to get near it.
—THE ERSATZ ELEVATOR

The bell of regret, I'm sorry to say, must ring.
—LEMONY SNICKET: THE UNAUTHORIZED AUTOBIOGRAPHY

"There are secrets everywhere.
I think everyone's parents have secrets.
You just have to know where to look for them."
—Quigley Quagmire, THE SLIPPERY SLOPE

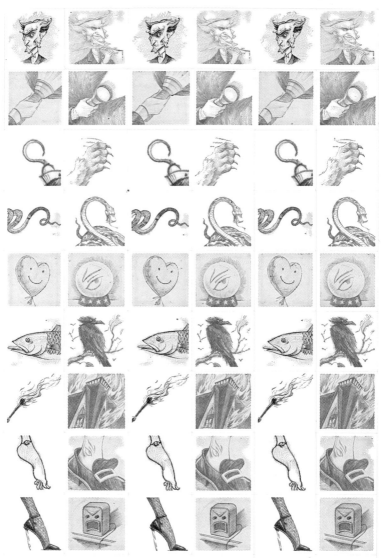

The world is quiet here.   The world is quiet here.   The world is quiet here.

A Creepy Mystery   A Creepy Mystery   A Creepy Mystery   Planka?

A Mysterious Creep   A Mysterious Creep   A Mysterious Creep

Plemo!   Unfeasi!   Krechin!   Gibbo!   SOS!   Egad!